Miss Hunt's Magic Map

By Jenna Grodzicki
Illustrated by Kevin Fales

Kelvin can't wait to get to school.
His class is taking a field trip!
But they aren't going on a bus.

Kelvin's teacher has a magic map.
It can take the class anywhere in
the world.

"We are visiting habitats today,"
says Miss Hunt. "Here we go!"

habitat: the home of an animal or plant

3

Poof! The class lands on an iceberg in the ocean.
Kelvin and his friends pull on their coats.

"Brrr," says Alex.

"Are we at the North Pole?" asks Nora.

"Yes, we are! The North Pole is a polar habitat," says Miss Hunt.

A polar bear and her cubs walk by.
Walruses slide off the ice and into
the water.
Kelvin sees a fox in the snow.

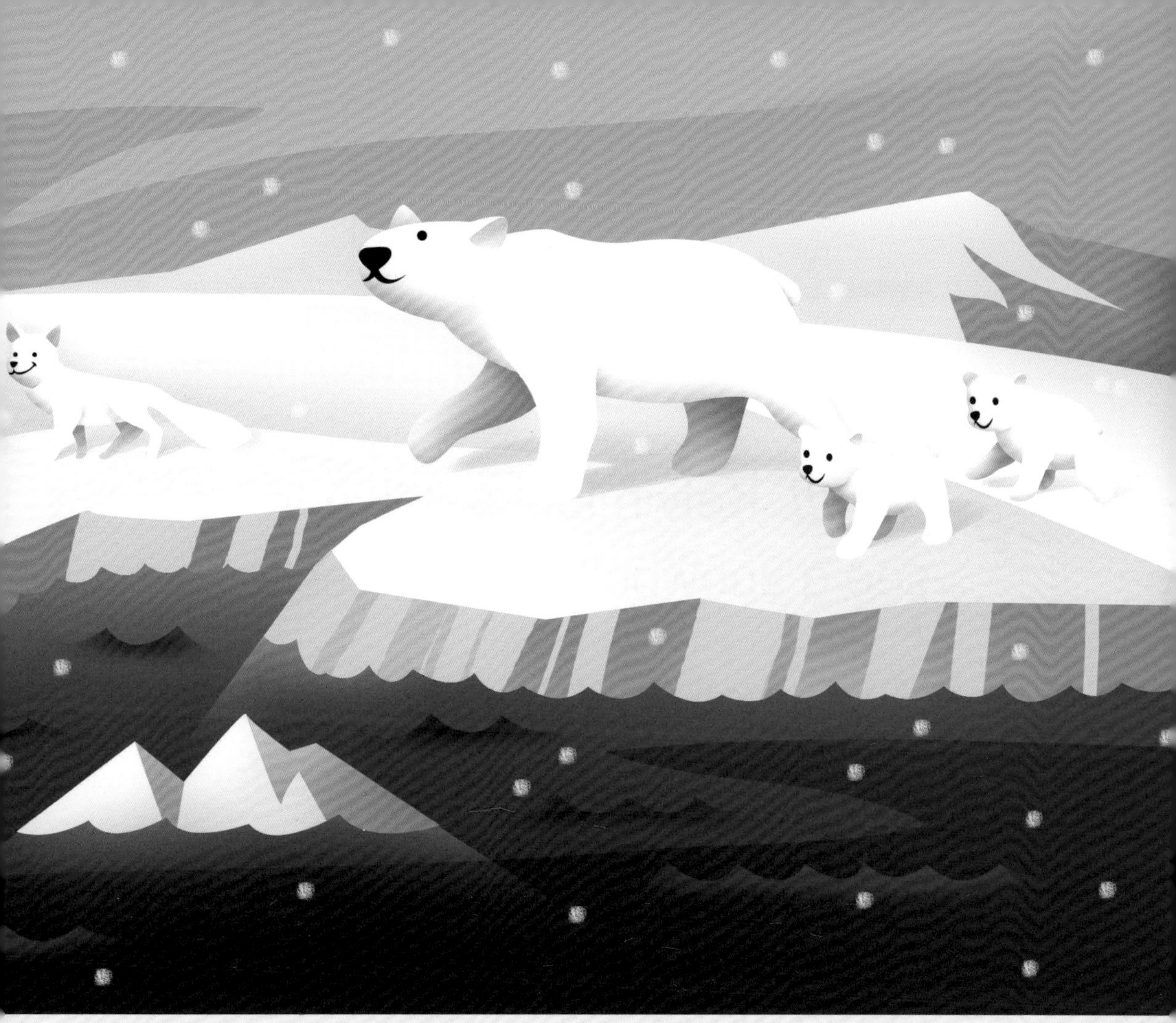

“They must be so cold,” says Nora.

“Polar bears and foxes have thick fur to keep them warm,” says Miss Hunt. “Walruses have blubber.”

Splat! Kelvin looks down to see a snowball hit his chest.

"Snowball fight!" yells Alex.

Everyone laughs.

Just then, a whale jumps out of the water.
"We're going to get splashed!" yells Kelvin.

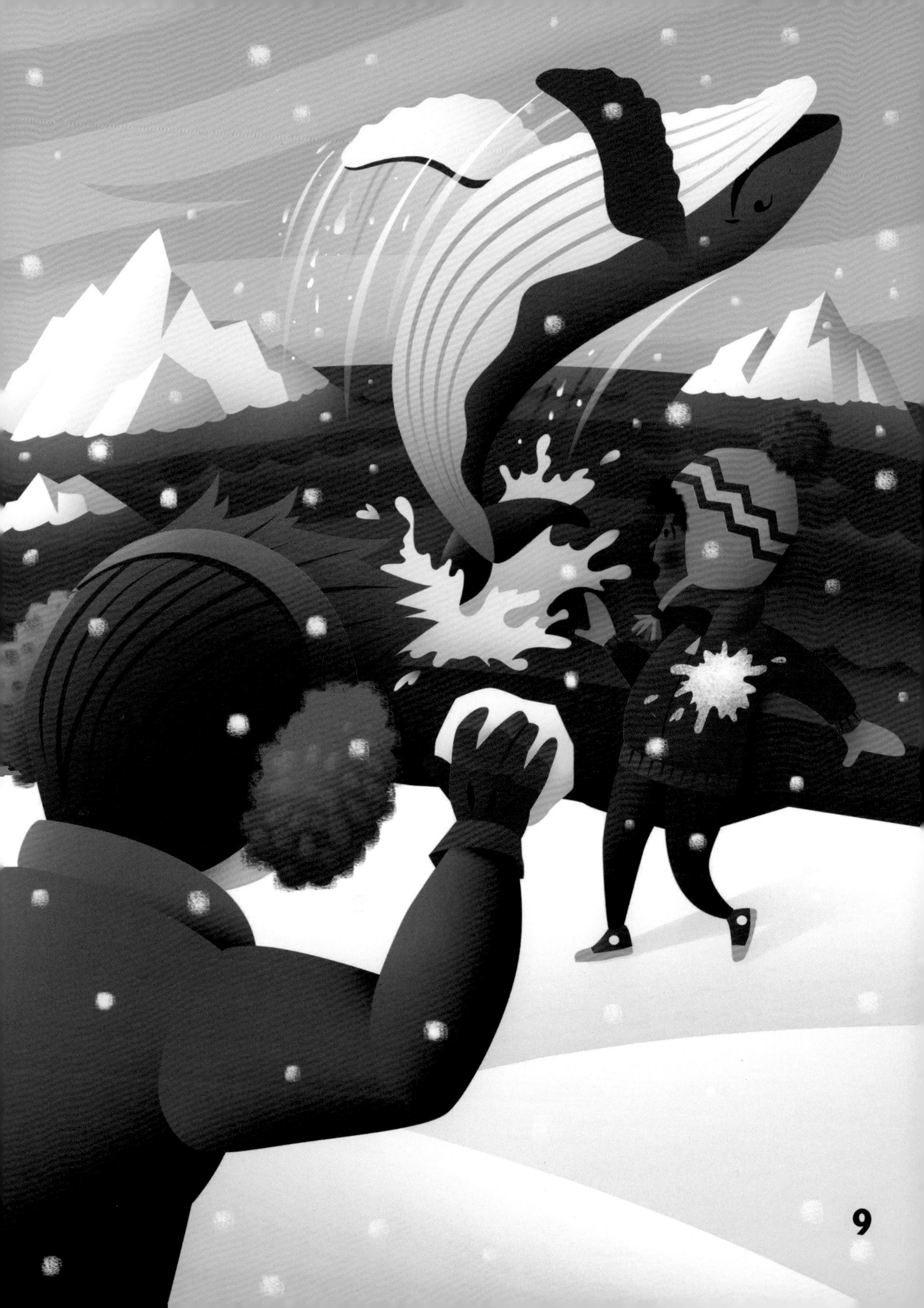

Miss Hunt pulls out the map.
"Time to go!" she says.

Poof! The class lands
in a rain forest.
Tall trees stretch to the sky.

Kelvin and his friends take off
their jackets.

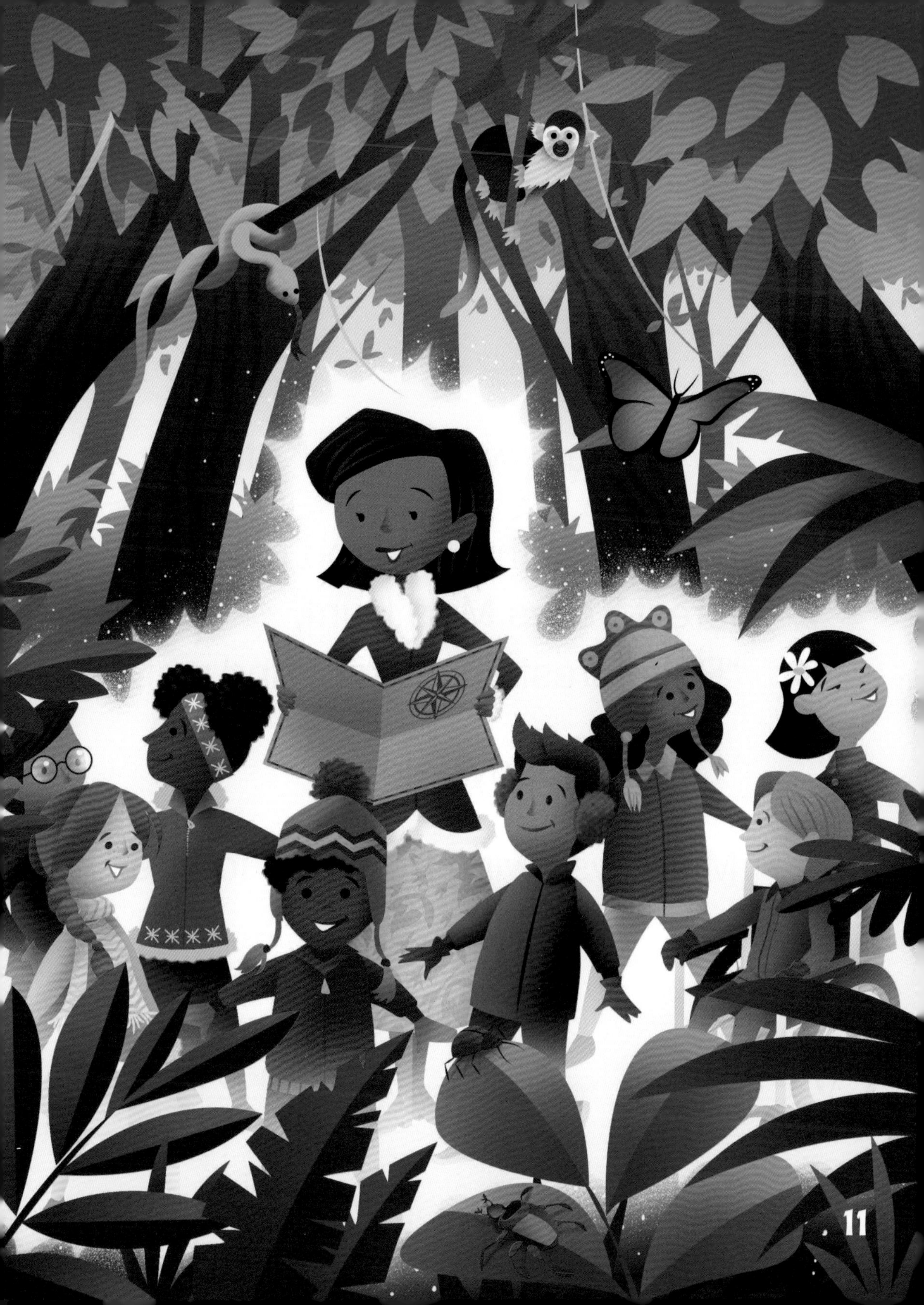

"Where are we?" asks Kate.

"We are in the Amazon rain forest," says Miss Hunt.
"Rain forests are warm and wet."

"Look up," says Nora.

Monkeys swing from tree to tree.

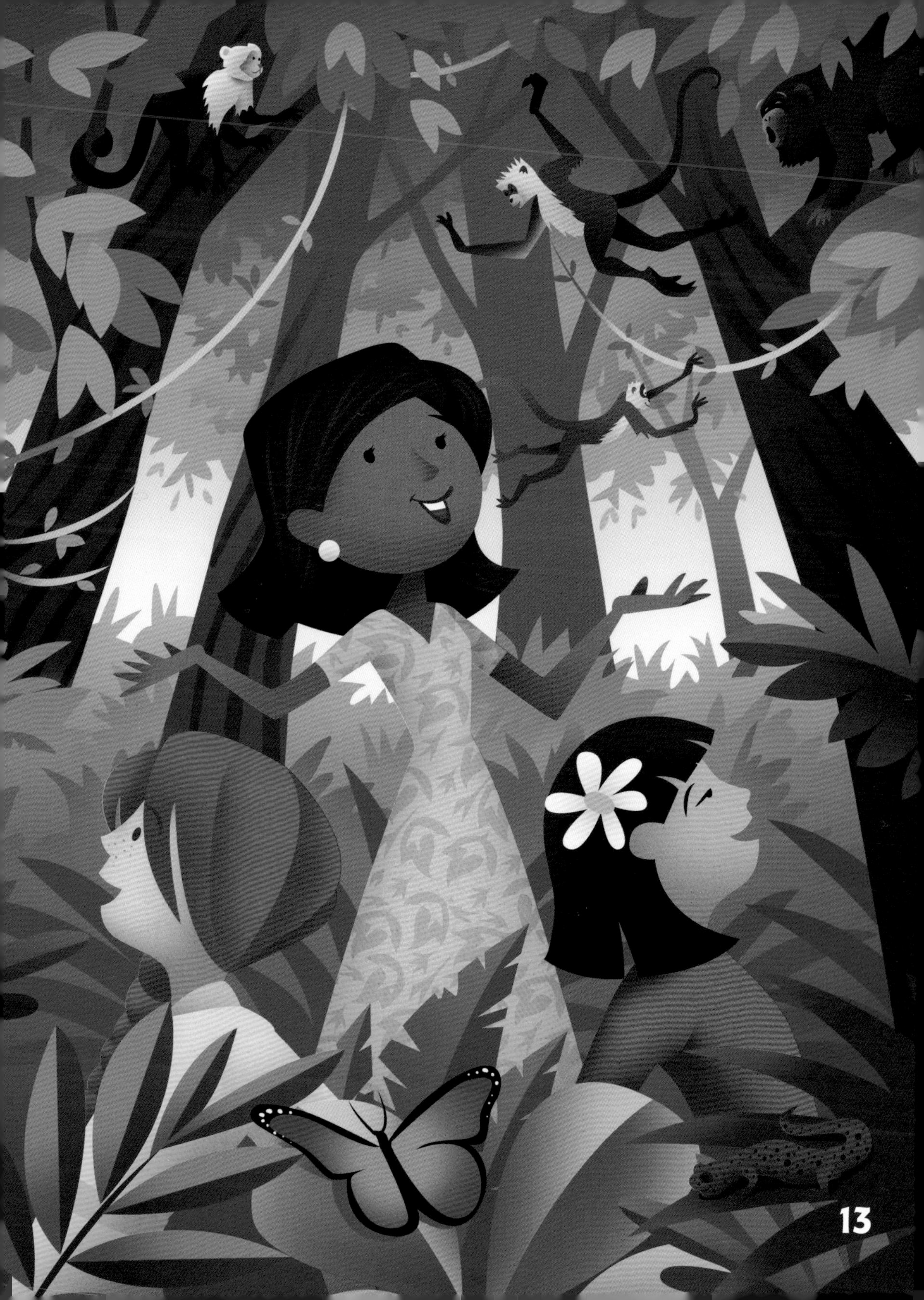

A butterfly flies by.
Kelvin spots a sloth hanging from
a branch above them.

"Rain forests are home to many
different animals," says Miss Hunt.

"It's so hot here," says Kelvin.

"These animals don't need thick fur or blubber," Miss Hunt replies.

Kelvin hears a soft *plip*, *plop* sound
as rain lands on leaves.

"It must rain a lot," says Kate.
"It is so green here."

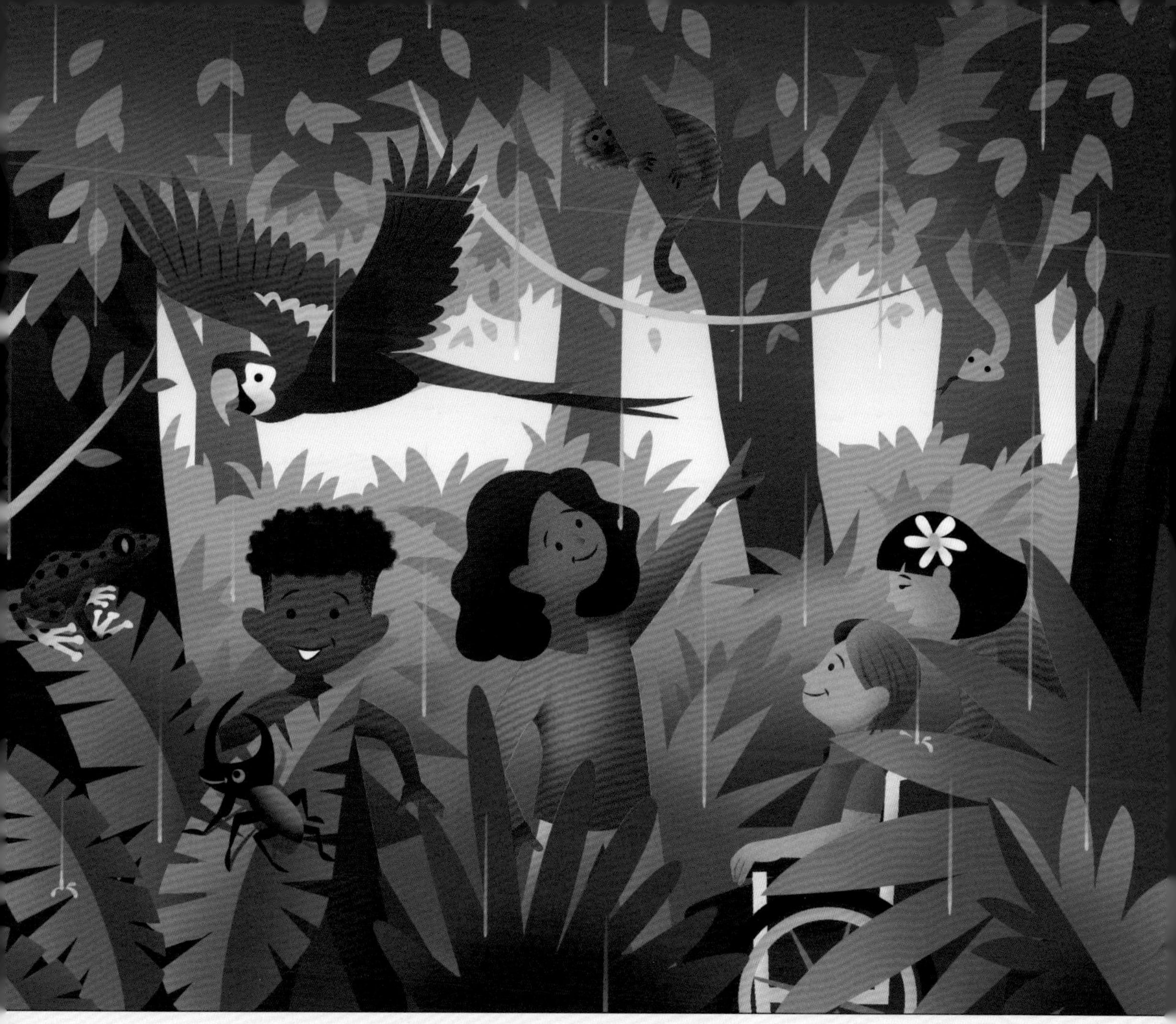

Alex leans against a tree.
He feels something hairy.
"Spider!" he screams.

"Let's go!" Miss Hunt says
and pulls out the map.

Poof! They are back at school.

"Miss Hunt, what's on your head?" asks Alex.

A frog hops off her head and lands on a desk.
Everyone giggles.

"Now, we need to take a field trip to the zoo," says Kelvin.

habitat: the home of an animal or plant

Consultant

Theresa Blue
Resource Specialist
Sierra Sands Unified School District, California

Publishing Credits

Rachelle Cracchiolo, M.S.Ed., *Publisher*
Emily R. Smith, M.A.Ed., *VP of Content Development*
Véronique Bos, *Creative Director*

Image Credits:
Illustrated by Kevin Fales

Library of Congress Cataloging-in-Publication Data

Names: Grodzicki, Jenna, 1979- author. | Fales, Kevin, illustrator.
Title: Miss Hunt's magic map / by Jenna Grodzicki ; illustrated by Kevin
    Fales.
Description: Huntington Beach, CA : Teacher Created Materials, [2022] |
    Includes book club questions. | Audience: Grades K-1.
Identifiers: LCCN 2020006570 (print) | LCCN 2020006571 (ebook) | ISBN
    9781087601366 (paperback) | ISBN 9781087619521 (ebook)
Subjects: LCSH: Readers (Primary) | Habitat (Ecology)--Juvenile fiction. |
    School field trips--Juvenile fiction.
Classification: LCC PE1119 .G786 2020 (print) | LCC PE1119 (ebook) | DDC
    428.6/2--dc23
LC record available at https://lccn.loc.gov/2020006570
LC ebook record available at https://lccn.loc.gov/2020006571

5482 Argosy Avenue
Huntington Beach, CA 92649
www.tcmpub.com
ISBN 978-1-0876-0136-6
© 2022 Teacher Created Materials, Inc.